FIC
WAT

Waters, Kate.

The mysterious
horseman.

11115
$15.95   06/06/1995

007214   11-111-11   504733

T H R O W A W A Y

C A R D

The Mysterious Horseman

An Adventure in Prairietown 1836

by Kate Waters Photographs by Marjory Dressler

SCHOLASTIC INC.

NEW YORK

Many thanks to all the staff and volunteers at the Conner Prairie museum, especially: Deb Cottrell, Steve Cox, Timothy Crumrin, Eddie Grogan, George Hoffman, Shannon Joines, Jan Kehr, Brenda Myers, Julie Olds, Joan Payne, Joe Roberts, Bonnie Shea, Nancy Stark, Karen Stubbs, and Jim Willaert.

Of course, our heartfelt gratitude to the cast: John Henry Olds, who is Andrew McClure; Jacki Masi-Razmus, who is Mrs. McClure; Bob Drew, who is Mr. McClure; Randy Payne, who is Thomas; Colleen Cox, who is Jenny; Mike Shultz, who is Mr. Curtis; Chris Sitler, who is Master Ferguson; Tom Lewis, who is Mr. Whitaker; Betty Watson, who is Mrs. Zimmerman; and Mikki Baird, who is the wagon driver.

Thanks also to Marijka Kostiw, Associate Art Director, for her immaculate care in the design of this book; and to Lynette Phillips, for her support during its creation.

Map on page 34 and woodcuts throughout by Heather Saunders.

"Yankee Doodle," p. 39, by Dr. Richard Shuckburgh, arranged by William Ward, is used by permission of Silver Burdett and Ginn.

For Dianne Hess
— K.W.

To my father, who gave me my first camera,
and to my mother, who inspired me to use it
— M.D.

Library of Congress Cataloging-in-Publication Data

Waters, Kate.
The mysterious horseman:
an adventure in Prairietown, 1836
by Kate Waters; photographs by Marjory Dressler.
p.   cm.
Summary: Andrew hopes for excitement
when his family moves from their farm to Prairietown in 1836,
but things seem pretty tame until
he overhears talk about a mysterious night rider.
ISBN 0-590-45503-6
[1. Frontier and pioneer life — Indiana — Fiction.   2. Indiana — Fiction.]
I. Dressler, Marjory, ill.   II. Title.
PZ7.W26434An   1994
[Fic] — dc20   93-31876
CIP
AC

12 11 10 9 8 7 6 5 4 3 2 1   4 5 6 7/9

Printed in the U.S.A.   37

First printing, September 1994

Designed by Marijka Kostiw

Andrew leaned against the fence and thought about the past year. So much had happened. But so far, Andrew wasn't sure that living in Prairietown was much better than living on the farm. He had spent three months helping Pa build their new house. Andrew's sister, Ada Noreen, had met James Cox at Mr. Whitaker's store and married him and moved away. And his baby brother, John Michael, had died of lung fever. Now, Andrew was the last of the McClure children left at home. Pa had told Andrew that he would see exciting things and meet exciting people in town. But Andrew had been so busy that it was even hard to find time to play with his new best friend, Thomas Curtis, who only lived down the road!

Today Pa had promised Andrew that he could be spared to work for Mrs. Zimmerman at The Golden Eagle Inn and earn some real money. He was saving the hard coin he earned there for a folding knife at Mr. Whitaker's store.

The sun came up this morning after all those days of
cold rain. The air was crisp, and people were anxious to start
putting by for the winter. Even Ma seemed more cheerful.
She had been awful sad since John Michael crossed over in
January. The house was sure quiet without the baby. And
Andrew thought she must be missing Ada Noreen, too.

Andrew had been quick with his dressing. This was a day
to be outside. Ma had tied his kerchief and told him the chores
that needed doing before he could go to work at the inn.

After breakfast, Andrew chopped wood so Ma would have enough for the day. He brought the last smoked ham out of the smokehouse. Stores were getting low. Soon it would be time to slaughter the pigs and smoke meat for the next year. Carefully, Andrew gathered eggs to bring to the store. He said good-bye to Ma.

Walking down the street, Andrew saw a wagon hitched up in front of the store. Some lucky family was heading west to the frontier! Andrew looked at the tall draft horses and the high driver's seat. Someday, he thought, I'll go west, too. Maybe I'll settle land or maybe I'll join the army and be like Davy Crockett.

Inside the store, Mr. Whitaker counted the eggs and made
a mark in his account book. Then, because it wasn't too busy,
he took out the folding knife and let Andrew look at it.
Andrew wished he could have the knife now, but he didn't
have enough hard coin yet. And Mr. Whitaker didn't give
children credit.

Finally, Andrew could go down the road to the inn. Mrs. Zimmerman kept a good, clean inn and people said she served the best food on the road west. When the road was passable, like today, the inn was always filled with boarders, and Andrew was sure to hear some interesting news.

Mrs. Zimmerman told Andrew what needed doing. And as she watched him sweep the kitchen, she told him *exactly* how she wanted things done. Mrs. Zimmerman was *very* particular.

Andrew gently curried the horses and carefully lifted fresh
hay into the stall.

Finally, it was time to sweep all the porches. This was the
best part of the job because you could listen to the travelers in
the taproom. It seemed as though they were all talking at
once. Andrew tried to sweep quietly. He could hear scraps of
their talk: "…the new road to Indianapolis…President
Andrew Jackson…the Alamo."

When Andrew finished, Mrs. Zimmerman offered him a cup of cold water. Now, he could finally sit down.

Mrs. Zimmerman wouldn't let children in the taproom when men were there, but Andrew crept as far as he could inside the doorway. Over the noise, Andrew could hear one man with a deep voice talking about a mysterious horseman and a poor schoolmaster. Andrew moved as close as he dared and listened hard. "...Night rider," he heard over the din. "...Some people say he doesn't have a head...comes out of nowhere...dressed all in black...chasing a poor schoolmaster..."

Andrew's hair stood up on his neck like the fur on a scared cat. Could the traveler really be telling the truth? Was the mysterious rider headed toward Prairietown? Did the rider have anything to do with the arrival of the new schoolmaster? Andrew held his breath.

Just then, Mrs. Zimmerman came out. "That's no talk for boys to hear, Andrew. Some of those travelers have had too many ardent spirits. Off you go." Andrew jumped up and went inside with her. His heart was pounding as she paid him. Andrew couldn't wait to tell Thomas what he'd heard!

He ran down the street toward the schoolhouse. He had to find Thomas and talk to him. Thomas's sister, Jenny, was washing the schoolhouse windows. That must mean that Mr. Ferguson, the new schoolmaster, had arrived and school would start soon.

"Where's Thomas?" Andrew asked.

"Inside helping," Jenny said.

Andrew rushed inside.

"And who are you?" asked the schoolmaster.

Andrew just stared and whispered to Thomas, "I have to tell you what I heard at the inn…."

As Andrew helped Thomas sweep the fireplace and set out the benches, Mr. Ferguson coughed. Andrew jumped. The schoolmaster wanted to talk to them! As they listened to him talk about winter classes, Andrew thought it sounded like more than letters and ciphering. Why did he need to learn rhymes and maps just to do business like his pa?

Andrew took notice of the time. Durn, he hadn't had time to tell Thomas *anything*! But he had best be home for midday meal. He told Thomas that he'd meet him later.

When Andrew ran into the house, he could smell the gingerbread Ma was mixing. "Go tell your pa that the meal is ready, son," Ma said. Andrew went out back to the workshop. He shivered when he saw that Pa was making another coffin. It looked so tiny. Pa was the only woodworker in town, so he did everything, from fixing cart and wagon wheels to making furniture. But making coffins was sad work.

The coffin most likely made Pa think of John Michael because his grace was long and slow and nobody talked much during the meal.

Afterwards, Ma looked so sad that Andrew asked if he could help with anything else instead of running to see Thomas like he wanted. Ma was putting apples by, so he helped her string them to dry above the fire. They would have pies and sauce all winter long. Andrew told his ma about the wagon at the store and about meeting the schoolmaster. In a while, Ma smiled and said he really should be off to find Thomas before the fish stopped biting.

In the yard, Andrew stopped at John Michael's grave. We miss you, he thought, as he cleared away some weeds that had grown up around the baby's gravestone.

Hurrying down the street to Thomas's house, Andrew thought about the horseman. Was he on his way to Prairietown? Is that why the men in the taproom were so excited? Was the rider a murderer? Or was he a spirit? And what about the new schoolmaster? Could he have anything to do with the story? Andrew couldn't wait to talk about everything with Thomas.

Thomas was waiting for him at his door. As they walked to the river, Andrew talked and talked.

At the river, they fished and built a fire. All of a sudden, it got very quiet. Andrew and Thomas listened. It seemed that even the birds were quiet. "He's coming," whispered Andrew. "I bet he's coming to Prairietown."

"We aren't getting any bites," Thomas said. "Let's go home."

The walk home seemed longer. Andrew and Thomas
walked close together. Then, Andrew heard sounds in the
distance. THUD, thud, thud. THUD, thud, thud. Andrew
held his breath. The sounds were coming closer.

"Let's run," said Thomas.

"Let's hide," cried Andrew at the same time.

Andrew and Thomas dashed to the side of the road and
crouched in the bushes. Something was coming down the road.
The ground began to shake. The birds in the trees were
startled and flew away. Andrew held his breath.

A dark shape thundered around the bend and down the road toward Prairietown.

Andrew and Thomas ran. They took the shortcut through
the graveyard, even though it was creepy. They jumped over
gravestones and sprinted through the woods toward home.

They got to Thomas's house first. There, they ran into
Thomas's father's blacksmith shop. When they could talk, they
told Mr. Curtis about the rider and the talk at the inn and
about the danger.

Mr. Curtis listened and told Andrew and Thomas to sit quiet and wait. Then he left. Was he going to get his gun? Was he going to warn the new schoolmaster? Should Andrew run home and warn Pa? Mr. Curtis walked back into the shop. But he wasn't carrying a gun. He was carrying a book. Andrew stared as Mr. Curtis sat down and began to read.

The dominant spirit, however, that haunts this enchanted region, and seems to be commander-in-chief of all the powers of the air, is the apparition of a figure on horseback without a head. It is said by some to be the ghost of a Hessian trooper whose head had been carried away by a cannonball in some nameless battle during the Revolutionary War, and who is, ever and anon, seen by the countryfolk hurrying along in the gloom of night as if on the wings of the wind.

As Mr. Curtis read, Andrew listened closely. The story was about a headless horseman and a poor schoolmaster. This must be the story he had heard at the inn. The traveler was talking about a new book, not about a real rider! Andrew was sure that the new schoolmaster must think he was pretty slow to have stared at him like that.

When it was dark, Mr. Curtis put the book down at an exciting part and sent Andrew home and Thomas into the house. Andrew went right to his pa and told him about the inn and the rider and the story in the book. Pa laughed. "Your 'mysterious horseman' was probably just the circuit rider, son. You'll see a lot more riders during the fall months. You'll get used to it."

Before bed, Pa read from the Bible.

When he was done, Ma kissed Andrew good night.

Andrew curled up on his bedding and listened to the sounds of the night. He could hear the chickens rustling in the shed, and the soft voices of Ma and Pa downstairs. And in the distance, he thought he could still hear the THUD, thud, thud, THUD, thud, thud of a horse's hooves.

Just before he fell asleep, Andrew had a feeling that tomorrow would be a good day, too. He might get to work at the inn again if Ma could spare him. Maybe the fish would be biting. And, best of all, maybe he would hear the rest of the story of the headless horseman!

Prairietown, Indiana, 1836

PATH TO THE WHITE RIVER

CURTIS HOUSE AND BLACKSMITH SHOP

POTTER'S

WHITAKER HOUSE AND STORE

McCLURE HOUSE AND CARPENTER'S WORKSHOP

SCHOOL

DOCTOR'S

WIDOWER'S

WEAVER'S

THE GOLDEN EAGLE INN

BARN

ABOUT CONNER PRAIRIE

Conner Prairie is a living history museum in Fishers, Indiana. One of the many features of the museum is an historically accurate recreated nineteenth-century village called Prairietown. It is composed of actual buildings from pioneer times. Although the buildings had originally existed in different parts of the state, the museum moved them to Conner Prairie.

Throughout the village, actors, called interpreters, act out life as it was in 1836. Visitors to the museum are free to walk in and out of the various buildings and talk to the villagers who go about their daily lives as they would have in 1836. They prepare period foods, shoe horses, do woodwork, mind the store, keep the inn, and care for the animals that graze in the fields.

Prairietown is a fictional town created by historians at the Conner Prairie museum. It functions as small towns in Indiana did at the time. Researchers created the characters the actors play by poring through available records. They looked for pioneers with the most interesting histories and backgrounds, then combined these aspects to create the characters and their histories. For example, the McClures are a composite of three different carpenters' families.

Based on historical facts, the following story lines of Prairietown and the McClure family accurately bring to life Indiana's first generation of settlers.

Prairietown, Indiana, 1836

In 1836, Prairietown, Indiana, was only four years old. It was founded by Dr. George Washington Campbell, an entrepreneur who purchased land in the area. He knew that people would not settle in and around Prairietown unless it had a store, a carpenter, a blacksmith, and a school. So he advertised in newspapers for mechanics (tradesmen) to settle in his new town. He also knew that thousands of people were pouring through the area to take advantage of the cheap land on the "new frontier" farther west. So Dr. Campbell built an inn where travelers paid twelve and one half cents a night for a bed.

Prairietown sat on the edge of the prairie above the banks of the White River. The soil was rich, and farmers thrived. People who shopped in Prairietown could buy almost anything that people in Boston or any other large city could buy. Mr. Whitaker, the storekeeper, rode four to six hours to Indianapolis every two weeks to stock up on staples like sugar, salt, and molasses. Twice a year he traveled for two days to get to Cincinnati to pick up goods like cloth, china, books, and candles.

Mr. Whitaker's store accepted hard coin, goods and services, and produce as payment. It was common in the community to be paid in services instead of money. Mr. McClure often received wool or chickens, or services like shoeing a horse, in exchange for the woodworking he did.

In 1816, Indiana became the nineteenth state to join the Union. It was a time of great patriotism and growth in America. The building of roads and canals was increasing. During this time, Andrew Jackson was the President of the United States. Americans were full of hope, and felt that prosperity and good times were ahead.

The McClure Family

The McClure family was of Scottish–Irish descent. Andrew's great-great grandfather came from Ireland to Virginia as an indentured servant. Andrew's mother, Hannah Jane, was Mr. McClure's second wife. His first wife died in childbirth.

In 1830, the family had traveled from Ohio to Indiana along the National Road. The National Road was the first road constructed by the government. By 1836 it ran from Cumberland, Maryland, to Vandalia, Indiana. It was almost completely straight and was covered with a surface of crushed stone.

When the family first arrived in Indiana, Mr. McClure tried to farm with his uncle. However, when his uncle died, Mr. McClure used the money he inherited to buy land and several buildings in town. He had seen Dr. Campbell's advertisement and felt that there would be more economic opportunities in town for his family. And Mr. McClure really wanted to be a full-time carpenter.

Andrew's main function was to run errands for his mother and to supply her with what she needed every day: water from the pump and wood. But his days were not all work. He had time to play with friends and visit neighbors.

Andrew's dreams centered around the glory of the Republic. Like most Americans at the time, Andrew was very patriotic. His heroes were Davy Crockett and George Washington. His favorite song was "Yankee Doodle."

School

The school of Prairietown was a subscription school. That means the town paid an average of three cents a day for each child to attend. The money paid the schoolmaster's salary and provided for supplies and firewood. The schoolmaster was housed by different families in town.

School was usually held only in December, January, and February. During the other months, children were busy helping their parents plant, harvest, and put by for the winter. But when school was in session, children went to school six days a week, from about 7 A.M. to 4 P.M. They learned by what is known as the "loud method" — facts and figures were repeated out loud over and over. Children of all ages did their schoolwork in the same room.

Washington Irving and "The Legend of Sleepy Hollow"

Washington Irving published "The Legend of Sleepy Hollow" in 1819–20. It was one of two short stories in a book called *The Sketch Book of Geoffrey Crayon, Gent. The Sketchbook*, as it is known, was first published in Europe where Irving was living. It made him famous in Europe and in the United States.

Washington Irving was one of America's first famous authors. (Another was James Fenimore Cooper.) Irving's stories were told and retold around hearth fires and camp fires across the country. The story of poor Ichabod Crane and the headless horseman quickly captured people's imaginations, including Andrew McClure's in the story.

About John Henry Olds

John Henry Olds, who acts the part of Andrew McClure in this book, was ten years old and in fourth grade when the photographs for this book were taken. He lives in Indianapolis, Indiana, not far from the Conner Prairie Museum.

John Henry and his mother volunteer at the museum. (His mother is the woman shopping in Mr. Whitaker's store.) He enjoys meeting people from around the world who visit the museum. He says he knows firsthand how much easier it is to live today than it was to live in 1836.

John Henry says that he really liked getting out of school early in order to be at the museum for the photography sessions, but he didn't like having to get up extra early on the weekends. He remembers that starting the fire by the river was hard because he had to use a piece of wool and a flint instead of matches. (Matches weren't invented yet!) And his favorite part of the photo shoot was riding in the Conestoga wagon.

Besides school and working at the museum, John Henry likes to spend his time swimming and Rollerblading.

Mrs. McClure's Gingerbread Recipe

Ingredients:

½ cup of butter
1 cup of sugar
1 egg
1 cup of molasses
1 cup of sour milk (milk with one drop of vinegar in it)
1 teaspoon of baking soda
1 teaspoon of ginger
3 cups of flour

Directions:

Add the sugar to the butter and mix well.
Beat the egg and add it to the sugar mixture.
Add the molasses.
Mix the sour milk and the baking soda.
Add it to the mixture.
Then add the ginger and the flour slowly.

Preheat the oven to 350 degrees Fahrenheit.
Pour the batter into a 9 inch greased pan.
Bake for 30–40 minutes or until firm.
(The cooking time will depend on how deep your pan is.)

Andrew McClure's Favorite Song

"Yankee Doodle" has been popular in this country since colonial days. The tune is very, very old. At first, the song was sung by the British to make fun of American soldiers. But the soldiers liked the song so much, they began to sing it, too!

YANKEE DOODLE

WORDS BY DR. RICHARD SHUCKBURGH
TRADITIONAL MUSIC

And there we saw a thousand men,	And there was Cap'n Washington,	He got him on his meeting clothes
As rich as Squire David;	And gentle folks about him;	Upon a slapping stallion,
And what they wasted ev'ry day,	They say he's grown so 'tarnal proud,	He set the world along in rows,
I wish it could be saved.	He will not ride without 'em.	In hundreds and in millions.

Chorus   *Chorus*   *Chorus*

GLOSSARY

THIS BOOK BELONGS TO

_____

WOODSON

The Adventures of
Bella & Harry
Let's Visit Rome!

Written By
Lisa Manzione

Illustrated By
Kristine Lucco

Bella & Harry, LLC

www.BellaAndHarry.com
email: BellaAndHarryGo@aol.com

"I am a gladiator!

I am a gladiator!"

5

"**Harry**, who are you talking to?"

"I am practicing, Bella. I am a 'Roman Gladiator'!"

6

"**Harry**, gladiators have not been around for thousands of years. A long time ago, gladiators were a part of competitions that were held in large areas, usually with a crowd watching the competition. Today Harry, gladiators can only be found posing for pictures outside the Roman Colosseum or in history books."

"**Where** is the Roman Colosseum, Bella?"

"The Roman Colosseum is in Rome, Italy. Remember, Harry,
we visited Venice, Italy with our family earlier this year.
Italy is in Europe. A lot of people think Italy looks like a boot!

Let's look at the map before we get started.
See Harry, Rome is here."

"Yes, Bella, I see Rome and I think
Italy still looks like a boot!"

"I agree Harry, but Italy is a very fancy boot!"

PORTUGAL   SPAIN

ROME

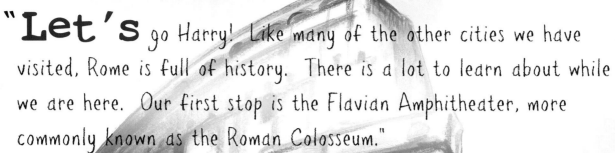

"**Let's** go Harry! Like many of the other cities we have visited, Rome is full of history. There is a lot to learn about while we are here. Our first stop is the Flavian Amphitheater, more commonly known as the Roman Colosseum."

"**Today**, the Colosseum is one of the most visited sites in Rome. The Colosseum is in ruins now, mostly because of earthquakes and stone robbers. There is not much left of the original floor, but you can still see the 'hypogeum' from the inside of the Colosseum."

"**Bella**, what is a 'hypogeum'?"

"A 'hypogeum' is an area underground. If you were a gladiator Harry, this is where you would have entered the stadium for your contest."

12

"**Most** people believe the Colosseum is one of the best buildings ever built by the Romans. The building is about 2,000 years old. It's an 'amphitheater', which means the building is usually oval or round, and there is no roof covering the center area of the theater."

13

"**Look** up there! That area is called Palatine Hill. Palatine Hill is one of the oldest areas in Rome. It is also one of the seven hills that Rome was built on. If you look below the hill, you will see the Roman Forum."

"We are going to the Roman Forum next. Come on, let's go!"

"**First**, the Roman Forum was a marketplace. Later Harry, many other buildings were built in and around the Roman Forum area during ancient times."

"**There** were all sorts of meetings held at the Roman Forum for both work and fun. Today, the Roman Forum is only ruins, but it too is one of the oldest areas of Rome."

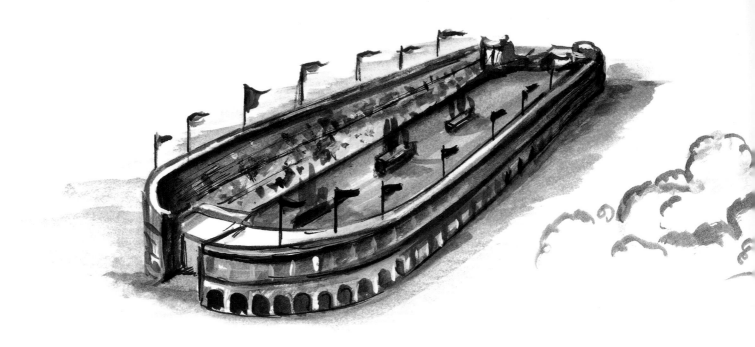

"**Next** stop, Circus Maximus!"

"Yay! I love the circus!"

18

"Harry, Circus Maximus is not a circus with animals or games. Circus Maximus was a place for chariot races long ago. It was the first and largest stadium in old Rome. It measures about 2,050 feet long ... or about 342 average lions ... standing tail to tail. It's now a public park."

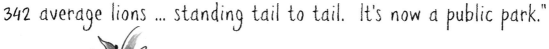

"**Lunch** time! We are going to have lunch at Piazza Navona today. The piazza, or open square, has a big fountain, which has one obelisk (a four sided, tall stone) in the middle of the fountain."

"**There** are two more fountains at each end of the piazza. Also, there are a lot of places in the piazza that serve lunch and dinner."

"**It** looks like the antipasto (or first course) includes cheeses, meats, and olives... you know, all of your favorites!"

"Yummy!"

"**Let's** go Harry! It's time to see a famous fountain and toss a coin in the water!"

24

"**Harry**, this is the Trevi Fountain, or Fontana di Trevi. It is the largest and most famous Baroque (a type of design) fountain in Rome. I am going to turn around and toss this coin in the water.

Harry? Harry?"

25

"**Harry**, what are you doing? Get out of the water!"

"**Bella**, look at all of the coins I found!"

"Harry, no! People toss coins in the fountain because legend says
if you toss a coin in the water, you will be sure to return to Rome.
We must come back to Rome, so leave the coins in the water.
There is so much more to see in this fun city! I am sure
everyone who tossed a coin in the water wants to come
back for another visit too!"

"Okay, Bella."

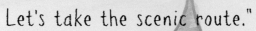"**Harry**, it's time to start walking back to our hotel.

Let's take the scenic route."

"**Harry**, we are now in an area called the 'Trident', which has lots of shopping and restaurants. Most of the streets in this area start with the name 'via', which means 'by way of' in our language."

29

WOODSON

"**Last** stop... the Spanish Steps! The Spanish Steps is a favorite location of both visitors and locals because of its beauty."

30

"The Spanish Steps make up the longest and widest staircase in Europe and they connect the lower piazza (Piazza di Spagna) with the upper piazza (Piazza Trinità dei Monti). Our hotel is located in the upper piazza, next to a beautiful old church. Let's race to the top!"

31

Whew! What a race! We are at our hotel at the top of the Spanish Steps. Harry and I are going to rest for a while after our fun tour of Rome. We can't wait for our next adventure but for now it's good-bye or "arrivederci" from Bella Boo and Harry too!

Our Adventure to Rome

Bella and Harry at the Pantheon.

Harry and Bella with the Vatican's Swiss Guard.

Bella and Harry enjoying spaghetti and meatballs.

33

Bella and Harry at the Vatican.

Fun Italian Words
and Phrases

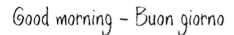

Yes – Si

No – No

Family – Famiglia

Good morning – Buon giorno

Good evening – Buona sera

Good night – Buona notte

Library of Congress Cataloging-in-Publications Data is available

Manzione, Lisa

The Adventures of Bella & Harry: Let's Visit Rome!

ISBN: 978-1-937616-08-3

First Edition

Book Eight of Bella & Harry Series

For further information please visit:

www.BellaAndHarry.com

or

Email: BellaAndHarryGo@aol.com

CPSIA Section 103 (a) Compliant

www.beaconstar.com/ consumer

ID: L0118329. Tracking No.: MR210171-1-10823

Printed in China